The Lion
and the Mouse

First published in Switzerland under the title *Der Löwe und die Maus*

No part of this publication may be reproduced in whole or in part, or stored in a retrieval
system, or transmitted in any form or by any means, electronic, mechanical,
photocopying, recording, or otherwise, without written permission of the publisher. For
information regarding permission, write to
North-South Books, Inc., 1123 Broadway, Suite 800, New York, NY 10010.

ISBN 0-439-26574-6

Copyright © 2000 by Nord-Süd Verlag AG, Gossau Zürich, Switzerland.
All rights reserved.
Published by Scholastic Inc., 555 Broadway, New York, NY 10012,
by arrangement with North-South Books, Inc.
SCHOLASTIC and associated logos are trademarks and/or registered
trademarks of Scholastic Inc.

12 11 10 9 8 7 6 5 4 3 2   1 2 3 4 5 6/0

Printed in the U.S.A.   14

First Scholastic printing, February 2001

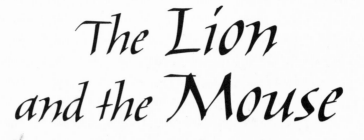

The Lion
and the Mouse

AN AESOP FABLE RETOLD
AND ILLUSTRATED BY

Bernadette
Watts

SCHOLASTIC INC.

New York Toronto London Auckland Sydney
Mexico City New Delhi Hong Kong

The lion cubs played happily in the sunshine while their parents slept nearby. The day grew hotter and hotter, so hot that the cubs grew tired. One by one they lay down to rest in the shade near their parents. Only one of the cubs kept on playing despite the heat.

When the blazing sun was at its highest, however, it was too hot even for him, so he padded over to a shady spot at the edge of the jungle and went to sleep.

Suddenly, a little mouse scampered across the sleeping lion cub's paw, tickling him and waking him up. The lion cub snarled angrily.

The mouse froze—too terrified to run away. "I'm sorry I woke you," she said, trembling.

When the lion saw that it was only a harmless little mouse, he smiled and said, "Off you go, little one. I won't hurt you."

"Oh, thank you for sparing my life!" said the mouse. "One day I will repay your kindness. If you ever need help, send for me."

The lion laughed out loud. "I am much bigger and stronger than you!" he said. "And soon I shall be even bigger and stronger. A mouse cannot help a lion."

Then the lion stood up and stretched to show just how big and strong he was. Proudly, he walked away.

The mouse ran in the other direction.

Years passed, and the cub grew into
the biggest and strongest of all the lions.
He was now the king of the beasts.

The days were long and hot, and every day at
noon the great lion would go to sleep in the shade.
If the mouse happened to run by, she kept well
away from the lion's paws.

One day when the lion headed for his resting spot, he fell into a trap! The more he struggled to get free, the more he entangled himself in the net.

The king of the beasts was caught! He gave a mighty roar. He roared with rage. He roared in fear. Then he roared for help.

The animals of the day heard his call and rushed up to him. But they couldn't help.

Night fell, and the lion was still trapped in the net.
The animals of the night crept up to see the captured
lion. But they couldn't help him either.

Early the next morning, the mouse appeared.
"You called for me?" she asked. "I will help you,
as I promised I would years ago."

The lion looked at the mouse in amazement.
"No one can help me," he said. "Least of all you."

The mouse started nibbling through the cords of the net, one after another. "Be patient, Lion," she said. "Soon you will be free."

Before long the mouse had chewed a hole in the net, and the lion pushed himself through it.

The lion was free! He stood before the mouse and bowed his head. "Thank you, little mouse," he said. "I will never again laugh at someone weaker or smaller than myself. To repay your kindness, I promise I will always protect you."

And so the lion and the mouse remained the best of friends until the end of their days.